KAYE UMANSKY
I Am a Tree

illustrated by Kate Sheppard

A & C Black • London

Thank you, Perse Prep School –
this is for you.

First published 2006 by
A & C Black Publishers Ltd
38 Soho Square, London, W1D 3HB

www.acblack.com

Text copyright © 2006 Kaye Umansky
Illustrations copyright © 2006 Kate Sheppard

The rights of Kaye Umansky and Kate Sheppard to be
identified as the author and illustrator of this work respectively
have been asserted by them in accordance with the
Copyrights, Designs and Patents Act 1988.

ISBN: 0-7136-7813-5
ISBN: 978-0-7136-7813-0

A CIP catalogue for this book is available from the British Librar

All rights reserved. No part of this publication may be reproduce
in any form or by any means – graphic, electronic or mechanica
including photocopying, recording, taping or information storag
and retrieval systems – without the prior permission in
writing of the publishers.

This book is produced using paper that is made from wood grown
managed, sustainable forests. It is natural, renewable and recyclabl
The logging and manufacturing processes conform to the
environmental regulations of the country of origin.

Printed and bound in Great Britain by Bookmarque Ltd, Croydo

The Cast

THE KIDS

Me – A tree
Flora Ferguson – A leaf
James Shawcross – Robin Hood
Charlotte Francis – Maid Marion
Wendy Wallace – Handmaiden 1
Shanti Kitimuru – Handmaiden 2
Fatima Lewis – Handmaiden 3
Little Thomas Kite – Little John
Ben Okobi – Will Scarlet
Rakesh Patel – Alan Adale
Sean Boyle – Friar Tuck
Dillon Gordon – Sheriff of Nottingham
Josh Mahoney – Prince John
Tariq Azziz – King Richard the Lionheart
Zoe McDonald – Peasant 1
Rachel Moss – Peasant 2
Karl Kaplinsky – Peasant 3
Jason Shaw – Peasant 4

THE TEACHERS

Mr Cunningham – head teacher and playwright
Mrs Axworthy – director
Miss Joy – music
Miss Steffani – dance and fighting
Mr Huff – backdrop and interval drinks
Old Mr Turnbull – keeper of order

TIM'S FAMILY

My mum
My dad
Kenny, my little brother

THE ANIMALS

Alf, our cat
Duke the rottweiler

Chapter One

I'm a tree! I thought, as I walked slowly home, feet dragging and heart in my boots. *A tree! They've cast the school play and I'm a tree!*

I was in shock. I couldn't believe it. I always get a good part. I'm great at drama. I'm an ace actor.

A *tree?*

I had gone and tackled Mrs Axworthy, of course, right after the list went up. I thought there had been a mistake. Well, there had to be. Me? Timothy Brown? The shining light of the school drama club? A *tree?*

'Excuse me, Mrs Axworthy,' I said, almost tripping her up as she came bounding out of the staff room.

'Yes, Tim?' said Mrs Axworthy, looking at her watch, clearly in a hurry. 'What is it?'

'I've just seen the cast list for *Robin Hood.*'

'Yes. And?'

'I'm down as a tree.'

'Yes. And?'

'Well, I thought…'

'Yes?'

'I thought, maybe, you'd made a typing error.'

'I don't think so. I know how to spell tree.'

'No, I mean…' Oh well. Might as well say it. 'I mean I auditioned for Robin. Failing that, the Sheriff of Nottingham. Or Friar Tuck.'

'Yes. And?'

'It says James Shawcross is Robin and Dillon's the Sheriff. And Sean Boyle's Friar Tuck.'

'Yes. And?'

A little silence fell, while the shocking truth slowly sunk in.

'So I didn't get any of them.'

'No. Look, I know you're good, Tim. *You* know that. We *all* know that. But you can't always have a starring role, you know.' Mrs Axworthy was rummaging in her handbag for her car keys. 'We have to give everyone a chance, don't we? You were God in *Noah's Ark* last year, after all.'

Yes, I was. And a jolly good God I'd been, too. I was in a sheet on a rostra block, towering over everybody, wagging my flowing beard,

our road, in the corner house. She wears glasses and has her hair scraped back with an elastic band. She has braces on her teeth too, and her mum buys her weird shoes with buckles.

Flora's all right, actually. She helped me make my beard when I was God last year. And came up with the idea of the cloud megaphone. (We are expected to provide our own costumes, unless there's something suitable in the school dressing-up box.) What would she say if she knew I was a tree? What a comedown.

'Hello, Tim,' said Flora. She spat some ice cream in my face. She can't help it – it's the braces. 'Sorry.'

'Hi,' I said, glumly, wiping it off.

'I hear you're a tree,' she said.

Oh. She knew.

'Mmm,' I said.

'I thought you tried for Robin.'

'I was going to,' I said. 'But then I thought about it. I felt I should let somebody else have a chance. I can't always get the main part. It wouldn't be fair. So I asked Mrs Axworthy to let me be a tree.'

'That was noble of you.'

'Yes,' I said. 'I know.'

'It's not true, is it?'

'No.'

We walked along the road in silence for a bit.

'I nearly drowned in a bowl of muesli this morning,' said Flora, suddenly.

'You did?'

'Yep. A strong currant pulled me in.'

Flora collects jokes. She was only trying to cheer me up. I gave a dutiful little chuckle. Then another silence fell.

'James Shawcross won't be as good as you,' she said, finally.

Too right he wouldn't. James Shawcross can't act his way out of a paper bag. I don't know why he goes to drama club. Probably for the orange juice and biscuits. He's good at learning lines. I'll admit that. It's just that he delivers them all bored-sounding, with no expression and hardly any pauses, like chanting multiplication tables. He's got a bleaty voice, too, like a sheep.

'No, no,' I said, airily. 'He'll be OK. A bit wooden, perhaps.'

'Not as wooden as you, though,' said Flora. 'You're a tree.'

How those words hurt!

'I expect you'll have a bull's-eye painted on you,' she went on, cheerily. 'The Merry Men will use you for target practice.'

Oh heck! I hadn't thought of that. She could well be right. I could accidentally get shot in the head with an arrow! Surely the school's health and safety regulations wouldn't allow it? I certainly hoped not.

'I do have lines to say, you know,' I said, slightly miffed.

'How many?'

'I don't know. Miss wouldn't tell me. Quite a few, though, I think.'

'I see Charlotte Francis is Maid Marion,' said Flora, looking at me sideways. She knows I've got a bit of a thing for Charlotte Francis, who has curly hair and socks with little stars on. I don't talk about her to Flora. They're not very friendly.

'Yeah,' I said, kicking a can. Then I whistled through my teeth a bit, in case she thought I cared. 'She'll be good.'

'I'm in the play,' said Flora, suddenly.

'You are?' I stopped in the road, feeling a bit guilty. I had been so anxious to find my own name, I hadn't taken in all the names on the cast list. Did Flora have a big, important part? Surely not. She doesn't like to open her mouth because of the braces. She's scared she'll spit and people will laugh. In assembly, if she has to say something, it's always an inaudible mumble.

'I'm a dancer. I do a leaf dance in the forest.'

'Oh, *riiiight*. Well – great.'

Now, don't spread this around, but personally I don't consider dancers to be very important. Dancing in a play is a waste of time, in my opinion. It's just there to give the girls something to do and kills time in between scene changes. I was about to dismiss it as something not worthy of more comment, when I suddenly remembered that I was a tree. They would more than likely be dancing around *me*. Oh, the shame!

'That's great,' I repeated, trying to sound upbeat. 'I'm sure you'll be very – leafy.'

We had reached Flora's house. She went in and I went on my weary way.

•

It wasn't a good evening. There were beans on toast for tea and Dad burnt the toast, setting off the smoke alarm. The only way you can stop it is to stand on a chair in the hall and wrap a towel round it. That's my job. By the time I managed to stop it, I was deaf as a post and my arms were dropping off.

Mum got home late because the car had broken down. She told us a long story about an AA man who she called a 'knight of the road'. Dad said he'd told her not to take the car until he'd changed the plugs. Mum said she'd wait 'til Doomsday if she waited for him. Then Kenny fell off his chair and cut his lip on the edge of the kitchen table. Kenny's my little brother. He can be very annoying, although I was sorry about his lip.

The TV was on the blink so I had no option but to draw a map of Australia, which I'd been putting off. I did it on the kitchen table, surrounded by blood, while Kenny wept and Mum and Dad argued about whether you should give an AA man a tip. I didn't mention that I was a tree. In fact, I kept very quiet, but nobody noticed.

After Australia, I played cars with Kenny, to console him after his lip incident. Then I read him a story about Chip the Potato, who loves diving into boiling fat. What kind of story is that for a two year old? Then I went to my room and read comics and stroked Alf until bedtime. Alf's our cat. He lives in my bedroom, to get away from Kenny.

My last thought as I drifted off with Alf purring away in my ear was: I'm a tree.

Chapter Two

We met in Mrs Axworthy's classroom, like we always do at the start of a play. Mrs Axworthy teaches Blue Class but takes on responsibility for all school productions, because she runs the drama club, of which I am a keen member.

She had a big sheaf of scripts on her desk. All the drama club members were there. Charlotte Francis was there, the stars on her socks twinkling away. So were Wendy and Zoe and Fatima and that lot. So was James Shawcross, and Little Thomas Kite and Dillon. And Josh, and Benny and Sean, and Tariq and Jason and Karl. Everyone looked flushed and excited. It's always fun when the parts get given out.

Well, it is usually.

Today, I felt more anxious than anything. Now was the moment of truth. I hoped it would be good news. I'd had a bad morning. Mr Huff hadn't been too impressed with my

Australian map, although I'd tippexed out the worst of the blood and sellotaped the tear (which Kenny did at breakfast). Mr Huff's my teacher. He's from Australia. That might have had something to do with it.

'Right,' said Mrs Axworthy. 'I've put your names on your scripts, so don't lose them. Thomas, dear, you're Little John, aren't you? And Benny, you're Will Scarlet...' And she proceeded to hand out the scripts to eagerly waving hands. 'Right,' she said, finally. 'I think that's all the speaking parts.'

'Um – excuse me?' I said, sticking up my hand.

'Yes? Oh, yes, Tim. The tree. How could I forget?' She picked up the last sheaf of stapled papers and handed them to me.

Hastily, I scrabbled through. Mrs Axworthy always marks our lines with yellow highlighter, to make them easier to read. I was on page 16 before I saw any. Yes! There they were! My lines! All four of them! They were written in rhyming couplets, of all things, and were as follows:

TREE: *So Robin and his merry men*
        As happy as can be
        Now spend a night carousing

Beneath the greenwood tree.

INTERVAL

Hmm.

Anxiously, I leafed through, looking for more yellow. Aha! Yes! There was another bit, on page 32, the last page. It was the final speech, the one that ended the play. All of two verses this time.

TREE: *And now the winter's over*
          And spring will not be long.
          O hark! The bells are ringing
          A happy wedding song.

          And so, farewell to Robin
          And his merry greenwood throng.
          How joyfully the bells ring out!
          Ding dong! Ding dong! Ding dong!

THE END

WHAAAAT?

'Right,' said Mrs Axworthy, briskly. 'Let's have a read through from the top. James, you start. *Act One, Scene One. Enter Robin.* Off you go.'

I peered over James's shoulder. His script was a riot of yellow. There didn't seem to be a single second when he wasn't saying something.

And I was a tree. A tree with nothing to say apart from a couple of rubbish remarks about carousing and weather and merry greenwood throngs before bursting into bell-speak. And it was all in rhyming couplets!

I stuck my hand up again, before James could start.

'Yes, Tim?' asked Mrs Axworthy, with a little sigh.

'I was just wondering who wrote the play this year, Miss,' I said.

Well, I was. Mrs Axworthy always does it. She does a pretty good job, too. She lets us add bits of our own, called improvisation, which is fun. She believes in teamwork. There are always plenty of jokes in our plays, which go down well with the mums and dads.

'Why?' asked Mrs Axworthy, sounding interested.

'Because – well, we don't usually do it all in rhyming cutlets.'

'It's not *all* in rhyming *coupl*ets. I take it you mean couplets, as opposed to lamb chops?'

This got a laugh from one or two, but went way over most people's heads.

'So who speaks in rhyming couplets, then?' I persisted.

'The tree does.'

'Only the tree?'

'Yes. Do you have a problem with that?'

'No,' I said, politely. 'I was just wondering who wrote it, that's all.'

Mrs Axworthy gave a funny little smile. 'If you really want to know,' she said, 'It was our very own Mr Cunningham.'

Mr Cunningham? Our head teacher? What was he doing writing plays when he should be busy ringing up celebrity chefs to come and improve our school dinners?

'Why not you?' asked Dillon.

'Because he suggested having a go this year. In fact, he was very keen. He's a bit of a playwright in his spare time, it seems.'

Did I detect a slight air of annoyance there? A tightening of the lips?

'I didn't think it was your style, Miss,' I said.

'No. Well, we all have different styles. Mr Cunningham has his own ideas. Apparently, he felt last year's *Noah's Ark* was a little … frivolous. I think that was the word he used.'

'What's frivolous mean?' asked Little Thomas Kite, who had somehow landed the part of Little John. Poor casting, in my opinion. Little John is huge, everyone knows that. Little Thomas is little. It defeats the point, somehow. I don't know what Mrs Axworthy was playing at.

'It means light hearted. Fun. He felt that Noah's ark was a serious subject. I don't think he liked the disco dance.'

'The disco dance was the best bit,' remarked Wendy (Handmaiden 1). She was right. The audience loved it. Some of the mums and dads got up and joined in!

'Well, I'm only passing on Mr Cunningham's comments,' said Mrs Axworthy. 'He feels the story of Robin Hood has a lot to teach us about social inequality. Less jokes and more education, in other words.'

'So we can't add funny bits?' asked Josh (Prince John).

'No. It's his vision. We mustn't interfere with a man's vision. We will perform it exactly as it flowed from the pen of Mr Cunningham. So if you have any comments about rhyming schemes, Tim, I suggest you run them past him.'

Not likely. You don't make negative comments to Mr Cunningham.

'Anyway,' went on Mrs Axworthy, 'I'd like to get started, if it's all right with you. Fire away, James.'

James finally found his opening line, and kicked off with as much animation as a plank. Well, a plank that bleats like a sheep.

'*Ho derry down derry fala lala la,*' he bleated. '*With a merry down dingle and a—*'

'That's a choir song. Don't bother with that,' cut in Mrs Axworthy. 'Start with "*Well, here I am, Robin Hood, hiding in the forest*".'

'*Well here I am Robin Hood hiding in the forest I*

wonder what I can eat tonight times are hard—'

'Excuse me?' I broke in.

James stopped bleating.

'Yes?' Mrs Axworthy sounded a bit weary.

'Is the tree on stage at this point?'

'Does it say so in the script?'

I consulted the script. It said: *SHERWOOD FOREST. ENTER ROBIN.*

'Not exactly.'

'Well, there you are, then.'

'But I should be, surely? It's a forest. I'm a tree.'

'Yes,' said Mrs Axworthy. 'I know you are.'

'So I'm there, then?'

'We'll have to see. Most of the action takes place in the forest. There may not always be room on stage, not when all the Merry Men are there. We may have to make do with the painted backdrop at this point.'

So not only did I speak in rhyming couplets, I was second fiddle to a painted backdrop!

'Can we get on?' said Mrs Axworthy. 'I'm sorry the stage directions are vague, but we can't help that, I didn't write them. The dinner bell will go shortly, I'd like to at least finish scene one. Carry on, James.'

James bleated on. There were an awful lot of lines in Robin's first speech and we were bored into a stupor by the time Little John arrived on page two to challenge him to a duel. Well, *I* was. I didn't think much of the lines Robin was given to say, but at least James could have tried moving his voice up and down now and then. *I* would have. I was dying to jump up, snatch the script out of his hand and put a bit of life into it.

But I couldn't, because I was a tree.

Little Thomas as Little John was a bit better. At least you could hear what he said and he attempted to put in some expression. But it was an uphill task, given the material he was working with:

ROBIN: *Challenge me to a duel would you?*
           Oh ha ha ha.
LITTLE JOHN: *I think you are afraid of this*
           big stick. I will win, you may be sure of that.
ROBIN: *Oh ha ha ha ha ha.*

'You're meant to laugh there, James,' said Mrs
Axworthy. 'You don't just *say* ha ha ha. You're
teasing him, in a mocking, merry sort of way.'

She wouldn't have had to tell *me* that. I knew
exactly how the laugh should go. It should be
accompanied by a twinkle and a slap of the
thigh. Or even an athletic leap, if space would
allow it.

'Oh, right,' bleated James. '*Ha ha ha ha ha.*'
It was an unconvincing laugh, like a sheep who's
just been told the world's corniest joke.

It went on. On page three, the script said:
THEY FIGHT

I imagined James and Little Thomas Kite
fighting. James is the tallest boy in our school,
with really skinny legs. Little Thomas is nine, but
has golden locks and appears about six. It would
look like a serious case of bullying.

'We'll skip that for now,' said Mrs Axworthy.
'Let's move on to Marion's entry, shall we?
Charlotte, the top of page four.'

26

script. Mrs Axworthy says we've got to stick to his vision.'

'Mr Cunningham?' Flora sounded shocked. 'I didn't know he wrote plays.'

'Well, he wrote this one.'

'Why? I thought he was too busy buttering up Ofstead Inspectors.'

'That's what I thought.'

'Is it any good?'

'Well, put it like this...' I said. And I went on to describe the 32 pages of turgid twaddle that was Our Leader's vision of *Robin Hood*. '...and then everyone sings a song with a lot of ding dongs and they're married and that's the end.'

We walked on.

'Heard about the two cannibals eating a clown?' said Flora. 'One says to the other, does this taste funny to you?'

I sniggered at that. Well, it was quite good.

That evening, the phone rang. I picked it up and said: 'Who's speaking, please?'

'You are,' said Flora, and rang off.

She can be a bit weird.

Chapter Three

Rehearsals began. Every day, at lunchtime. To be honest, I didn't enjoy them. It wasn't just that the play was no good and I was a tree. It was other stuff. Charlotte, for a start. Usually she's nice to me in drama club. We often get paired for improvisation and we work well together. But now she didn't seem interested in talking to me. She always sat next to James and Dillon and Little Thomas Kite and they tested each other on their lines. I knew my lines already, of course. Well, there was hardly a lot to learn.

Mrs Axworthy seemed a bit fed up too, as though her heart wasn't in it.

I did an awful lot of standing around, which I suppose was good preparation for being a tree. Although real trees don't have to endure watching a load of badly cast actors deliver badly written lines badly, which was all I seemed to do.

Things weren't going well. The Merry Men were about as merry as a bunch of undertakers. They couldn't raise a titter between them. Dillon's Sheriff of Nottingham sounded as menacing as Father Christmas. Prince John was no better. Friar Tuck, a part written for comedy if ever there was one, was as flat as a pancake. It wasn't really their fault. It was the script. The lines didn't *live*. They didn't *flow*. Some of the time they didn't even make sense!

Even Charlotte was struggling with Maid Marion. Mr Cunningham had written her as a medieval fruitcake. He gave her a lot of silly squeals and a morbid desire to dance all the time. If I were Robin, I would have run a mile. Her handmaidens were the same. Still, at least they weren't trees.

Until we started working in the hall, we had no idea of how much space we needed, so Mrs Axworthy never knew whether I should be present in a scene or not. I just played it safe. Whenever there was a scene set in the forest, I obligingly stood up and stretched my arms. Occasionally, just out of boredom, I would swish a bit, but nobody took any notice because someone else was always talking and I was just a tree.

Finally, the great moment arrived when we got to my first speech. As you know, it comes just before the interval.

'Right,' said Mrs Axworthy, trying to sound bright and positive. 'Tim's big moment. The tree speaks. Go for it, Tim.'

'Just a minute,' I said. 'Let me get in character. I need to think Tree.'

'Just get on with it.'

'*So Robin and his merry men*
As happy as can be
Now spend a night...'

I broke off. 'Look,' I said, pleadingly. 'Look, do I *have* to say this?'

'Don't start,' said Mrs Axworthy, clutching her head.

'It's just that nobody else has to speak in rhyming coup—'

'I know! I *know*! But that's how it's written. Say the stupid words and don't give me grief, all right?'

I said the stupid words. And I didn't just rattle them off, though that's all they deserved. I spoke them clearly and efficiently. I like Mrs Axworthy, even if she had made me a tree. The last thing I wanted to do was give her grief.

Mr Cunningham occasionally looked in on the rehearsals. When he did, things got worse than ever. People fell to pieces. They fluffed their lines and forgot everything they'd practised, like speaking up and not talking with your back to the audience. He never said anything. He just stood in the doorway, arms folded, listening and watching. Mrs Axworthy got in a tizzy, too. I know, because her neck went red. None of us liked it. We were always relieved when he went back to his office.

•

'So have you thought about your costume?' asked Flora. We were walking home. She was eating cheese and onion crisps. I was trying to stay out of accidental spitting range.

'No,' I said.

'Come round to mine tonight. I've got some cardboard and paint and stuff. I think we'll make a brown, painted cardboard tube for your trunk and droopy, green material to drape over your arms.'

'Have you got droopy, green material, then?'

'I'm a leaf, remember? You can have what's left over from my costume.'

'You've already made your costume?'

'Mum did. She insisted.'

'That was nice of her.'

'Mmm.'

'OK,' I said. 'Thanks. I'll come after tea.'

We're not good at things like costume making in our house. We're not equipped. We don't have things like pins or needles or glue. Kenny likes eating pins. He rolls in paint, too. Much better to go round to Flora's. Her mum's got a sewing machine. She makes a lot of Flora's clothes. Actually, I have to say they're not very nice clothes. They never seem to fit quite right. But you can't go wrong with sewing up seams on branches, can you?

Anyway, it hardly mattered what I looked like.

I was a tree.

Chapter Four

'This should work,' said Flora. We were in the living room. It's smaller than ours, with old-fashioned furniture. She was on her knees at my feet, pinning brown material around my legs. 'It'll give you more flexibility. You'll be able to bend your trunk in the wind. And your feet are free to kick away marauding rabbits.'

She was right. The brown material was better. We had tried the painted, cardboard tube idea, but it kept tearing when I tried to walk.

'Marauding rabbits?' I said. 'I didn't know trees were threatened by marauding rabbits.'

'Badgers, then. Squirrels. Whatever eats roots.'

'Warthogs eat roots, I think,' I said, although I didn't really know.

'Did they have warthogs in medieval times?' asked Flora.

'I think so. I know they had wolves.'

'There you are, then. You're safe from

ravening wolves. Woe betide any root-eating wolf who comes sniffing around *you.*'

'I'll kick him with my flexible feet,' I said. We were both giggling a bit.

'Perhaps I need an umbrella, in case of medieval acid rain,' I went on.

'Let's just hope there aren't any stray dogs,' said Flora.

We both rocked with laughter.

'Yeah,' I went on, spinning it out. 'If any stray dog comes near my flexible foot, I'll kick it right up the... Oh, hello, Mrs Ferguson – didn't see you there.'

Flora's mum had poked her head around the door. She walks with a stick. Something wrong with her leg, I don't know what. Flora's never said. She doesn't have a dad. I think he died or something, when she was small.

'Hello, Tim, how nice to see you. Would you like some lemonade and biscuits?'

'Yes please, Mrs Ferguson,' I said.

'Isn't it *exciting*?' she said, giving a little shiver.

'What?' I said. I like lemonade and biscuits, but I don't exactly get *excited*.

'The *play*!'

'Oh, right,' I said. 'That.'

I gave her a tired little smile, rolled my eyes a bit, and then waited. I expected her to go on to say how surprised and shocked she was to hear that I was merely a tree. I mean, she loyally turns out to all the school plays, even though Flora isn't in them and she doesn't have to. She knows my abilities in the acting department. She was one of the first to congratulate me on my God.

But she didn't.

'I can't believe Flora's in The Dance. I thought she'd be too shy. I didn't know what to say when she told me she'd auditioned and got in. I'm so proud of her. Only two weeks to go.

I'll have to get my best hat out for *that* night all right.'

'Right,' I said, vaguely. 'Yes, it's great, isn't it?' I glanced down at Flora. She had gone a bit pink.

'It's not *the* dance,' she said. 'There are lots of dances. I'm in one, that's all.'

'Yes, darling, but you're *in* it. That's the main thing. I'm going to see you *on stage*! And I always love the dancing. I was a dancer once, did you know that, Tim? You wouldn't know it to look at me now. But I think dancing makes a play, don't you? And this time I shall enjoy it even more because Flora's taking part. Shall I get your costume to show to Tim?'

'No, don't bother,' said Flora. 'He'll see it at the dress rehearsal.'

'Oh, all right. I'll just leave you to it, then.' And, beaming, she withdrew.

'That's the trunk pinned,' said Flora, standing up. 'I'll run it up later on the machine and paint a tree pattern on it. Do you think we should paint your face green? Or shall we make a mask?'

'Paint,' I said. 'I don't want my couplets to be muffled.'

'What about some sort of hat? I've got an old, green swimming cap. We could stick some boughs on it.'

'Made of what?'

Flora considered.

'Wire, covered with crepe. What d'you think?'

'Sounds good to me.'

I was happy to leave the decisions to her. She's quite arty. She draws great cartoons. I've seen them. They're mostly about ducks and an evil swan called Swan Hilda, who tries to take over the pond.

'Do you want a bird's nest? I can make one out of straw and sew it to your shoulder.'

'Why not? Let's live a little. All the best trees have shoulder nests.'

'Grey, cuddly squirrel? Or is that going a bit far?'

'A bit far, perhaps.'

'What about acorns? You can be a nut tree. We could stick on some cut-out acorns.'

'Acorns would be good. I'm nuts about acorns.'

'And I've got a couple of stuffed doves in the Christmas decoration box. We could paint them to be wood pigeons.'

'Bring 'em on!' I roared. 'Let's get this tree *decorated*!'

Her enthusiasm was infectious. I might be a tree, but by golly, I could still look good.

We had quite a fun time. We rummaged through boxes in the attic and experimented with face paints. Flora found her book with tree jokes in it and we read them out. Most were awful, but a few weren't bad. We cut material and glued stuff. When I left, at eight o'clock, the carpet was covered with bits of cotton and scraps of cloth and a big damp patch, where we'd spilled lemonade.

Mrs Ferguson didn't seem to mind. 'I'm glad you've had fun,' she said. 'I heard you giggling all the way from the kitchen. You must come again, Tim. Flora doesn't have many friends back.'

'I will,' I said. 'Thanks, Mrs Ferguson.'

She and Flora stood at the door and waved until I got to my house. Then they went in, to clear up. I felt a bit guilty. I should have stayed and helped.

Still, I now had a costume. It was pretty elaborate, too, what with the wood pigeons and the nest and the green material foliage and the extra boughs coming out of the swimming cap, not to mention the acorns. It filled a black bin liner. I was pleased with it.

When I got home, Mum was giving Kenny his bath and Dad was out in the garage fixing the car, so I put on some pasta and went to see if I could make the TV work. Sadly, I forgot the pasta, which stuck to the pan and set off the smoke alarm again. Mum came running down, with Kenny all wet and thrashing in her arms, while I tried to find a towel to shut the thing off. And Dad came in, grumbling that he'd banged his head on the underside of the car door. Mum suggested we get the AA to come and look it over, and there was another exchange of words about that.

I live in a mad house.

Chapter Five

I'm not going to go on about the acting rehearsals in Blue Class, which dragged on through a million dreary lunch hours. Suffice to say, we struggled through to the end, then started from the beginning again. And again. And again and again and again, until everyone knew their words. But it was still dull and uninspiring. Josh and Dillon did their best with Prince John and the Sheriff, hamming up the fist waving and trying to sound wicked and heartless, but they couldn't liven things up, because of the daft words they had to say.

Let's move on to the first time we did the stagger through in the hall. That's the theatrical term for fitting everything together. Actors, choir, orchestra and dancers. Everything except the backdrop, which Mr Huff was working on in his spare time, when he wasn't making sarcastic comments about maps of Australia.

The stagger through is always chaotic. There's never enough room on stage and people keep talking when they shouldn't. The choir's always got the wrong bit of music and the kid with the violin always breaks a string. The teachers get shrill, too. Mrs Axworthy is the overall director, of course, but she gets help. Miss Joy does the music. Miss Steffani trains the dancers. She also does the fight sequences, such as they are. In this case, there was only one, between Robin and Little John, and it was pathetic. It looked so unfair. You found yourself rooting for Little John, which isn't right, surely? I said as much to Charlotte Francis, who happened to be standing next to me, yawning and fiddling with her hair.

'Hilarious, isn't it?' I said, watching Little Thomas Kite feebly waving his stick at James's knees.

'What?'

'Those two.'

'I don't know what you mean.'

'Well – the height difference. James and Little Thomas. It's like a fight between Long John Baldry and a Munchkin.'

(Long John Baldry is an old, very tall, rock star. He is a favourite of my dad's. Mum prefers

Celine Dion.)

'Are you saying Thomas is short?' Charlotte looked at me with cold, grey eyes and curled her lip.

Oops. I had done it all wrong. The girls love Little Thomas. They love him *because* he's short. I think he brings out their mothering instinct.

'Well, yes. I mean, nothing wrong with that, but Little John is an ironic name, you see, he's supposed to be this massive great...'

I was talking to air. She had moved away to the radiator, to join her cronies. She said something to them, and suddenly every girl in the room was looking at me in a coldly critical way.

I tried again, when the Merry Men were doing their scene.

'Not very merry, are they?' I whispered, sidling up.

'What?'

'I said they're not very merry. Alan Adale looks like he's forgotten his sandwiches. And Will Scarlet looks like the dog ate his homework. And as for Friar Tuck…'

She had moved away again. All right. I got the message. She wasn't speaking to me. I was a tree.

When it came to my bit, I did it. I suffered, but I got on and did it. I stood there gamely waving my arms around while Marion and the handmaidens did their skipping dance around me. Shanti kicked me in the shin and Charlotte avoided looking at me the whole time, I noticed. They clearly hadn't forgiven me for my remark about Little Thomas.

'You don't have to hold your arms in the air the whole time, Tim,' said Mrs Axworthy.

'I expect they're aching, aren't they?'

'It's all right,' I said, nobly. 'I'm used to it, with the smoke alarm.'

She looked a bit puzzled, then told me to get out of the way because Robin and his Merry Men were on next and there wasn't room for me on stage. I thought this was ridiculous, having a tree go shuffling off in the middle of a scene, but Mrs Axworthy said there was no way round it.

I shuffled on again, to deliver the couplets which finished the first act. Then I was offstage for the next eight pages. On again so the peasants could dance around me. Off again, to make room for a load more people. On again so the leaves could do their bit. I was quite looking forward to the Leaf Dance so I could see Flora in fluttering action, but she was away that day, so I didn't have that pleasure.

Mr Cunningham came out of his office and stood in the doorway for part of that awful, rubbishy rehearsal. He just stood and watched. Then he went away again. You couldn't tell what he was thinking.

We ran through it all again the next day, and the next. And then –

Finally. The dress rehearsal. The bit that everyone enjoys.

There was still no sign of Flora, so I called in on my way to school. Her mum opened the door.

'Why, Tim!' she said, all pleased. 'How nice to see you.'

'Is Flora all right?' I asked. 'It's just that she hasn't been at school.'

'Bit of a tummy bug,' said Mrs Ferguson, adjusting her weight on her stick. 'Or else she's eaten something. And then I got it, I'm afraid, and she insisted on staying home to look after me.'

Poor old Flora. Three days in a house full of sick. I felt rotten. I should have rung her. I meant to, but somehow I never got round to it.

'It's the dress rehearsal for the play today,' I said.

'Oh no!' She gave a gasp. 'Is it? The play's not tomorrow is it? I must have written down the wrong date on the calendar! I thought it was Friday week.'

'No,' I said. 'Tomorrow.'

'Really? Flora!' Mrs Ferguson called into the house. 'Flora, it's the dress rehearsal *today*!'

There was a short pause, and then Flora appeared at her side. She had her book bag and a carrier bag, which I supposed contained her leaf costume. She looked a bit groggy.

'Are you all right?' I said.

'Yes,' said Flora. 'Fine.'

'Did you know it was today, darling?' asked her mum.

'Yes,' said Flora.

'I must have written it down wrong. You didn't tell me.'

'Sorry,' said Flora. 'I meant to.'

'Oh well, never mind. It makes no difference to me. I don't exactly have a lot on my social calendar. But you must have missed all the important dancing rehearsals.'

'It doesn't matter,' said Flora. 'It's not *Swan Lake*. We only leap about and flutter.'

'Hey!' I said. 'You'll be leaping and fluttering around me, remember?'

I was trying to make her smile. It didn't work.

We said goodbye to her mum, who stood in the doorway waving and wishing us good luck.

'Dance well, darling!' she shouted. 'I know you will. Take off your glasses! And don't forget to let your hair out! Use the band!'

'Looking forward to it?' I asked Flora, as we walked along the road, her with her carrier and me with my bin bag full of tree.

'No,' she said, shortly. 'I'm dreading it, if you must know.'

'Why did you audition, then?'

'Because of Mum. She was so keen for me to be in it this year. She never says much, but I know how disappointed she gets. There was no way I could act, but I thought she'd be pleased if I danced.'

'Well, she is,' I said. 'She's thrilled.'

'I know. But I hate it. I'm a terrible dancer. I'm taller than everyone else, for a start. And I've got huge, clumsy feet. Everyone else is small and dainty. And I have to leave my glasses off so I can't see properly. And I look awful with my hair out. Whenever the leaf music starts up, I get so nervous I think I'm going to throw up.'

'Well,' I said, 'if you do, try not to do it over my roots.'

I was still trying to cheer her up.

'All right,' said Flora, with a sigh. 'I'll aim for a marauding rabbit.'

'Got any new jokes?' I asked, just to keep things light. She didn't reply, so I guessed she hadn't. We were passing Mr Smallman's house at the time. He's got a big Rottweiler called Duke who always barks at us through the gate.

'Poor old Duke,' sighed Flora, sadly, as the barking started up.

'Why? What's wrong with him?'

'Haven't you heard? Mr Smallman took him to the vet because he's got crossed eyes. He was telling me about it. The vet picked him up and looked at his teeth, then his eyes. Then he said he'd have to put him down.'

'*Whaat*? Because he's got crossed eyes?'

'No. Because he's really heavy. Boom-boom!'

I laughed loudly at that. Flora gave a weak grin. She still looked pale, though.

•

The dress rehearsal was the sort of shambles that I have come to know and love so well. It's great seeing everyone else in costume for the first time, and having them make comments about you. My wood pigeons got a lot of attention. So did the acorns. Mrs Axworthy asked what the strange growth was on my shoulder, but saw immediately it was a nest when I told her.

Do you want to hear about the costumes? I'll tell you. Robin wore a green shirt, a hat with a feather and his sister Shirley's green, woolly tights. She's not as tall as he is, so he looked a bit uncomfortable. The Merry Men sported a selection of their mothers' old green jumpers and blouses, belted in. Will Scarlett's came from Top Shop. I know, because Mum's got the same one.

Friar Tuck wore a brown dressing gown with a cushion stuffed up it. The Royals wore a selection of curtains and crowns and the Peasants had straw hats. Marion's lot wore long dresses and wimples. And the leaves – well, they were also kitted out in a rag bag of green jumpers and tights and tracksuit bottoms. All except Flora.

Poor old Flora. Her mum had gone to town. It was a proper outfit, with a stiff skirt like ballet dancers wear. The top had been cut in a leaf shape, with jagged bits. In a way, it was a work of art. There were even embroidered veins. And there was a matching wafty scarf thing, which twined around her neck. But it didn't do a thing for her.

The leaf-shaped bodice cut in under her arms and the skirt was too short. Her green tights ended at the ankle, making her big feet really noticeable. Worst of all, she had let her hair out.

Holding it in place was a thick, green band with a weird bow on it. She really stuck out amongst the other leaves. Like some sort of invasive growth. She had taken off her glasses, as her mum had instructed, but I have to say she looked better with them on.

We have assemblies about kindness in our school. Nobody said anything when she came trudging in, head down, face crimson. Well, nobody except Charlotte. She gave a loud, sniggering laugh, behind her hand. Everyone heard it.

I couldn't look at Flora's face. No wonder she had been off sick.

Like I said, the rehearsal was a mess, because everyone was overexcited. The scenery was up now – a backdrop of Sherwood Forest, which transformed into the inside of Prince John's castle when turned round. The lights had arrived, too. Everything was happening at once and it was all too much. Everybody was giggly and silly and forgot everything they had practised. The teachers were in a panic as well. Miss Joy spilled her tea over the piano and Mrs Axworthy and Miss Steffani shouted a lot.

Mr Cunningham came to watch for a bit. When he was around, we all calmed down and got on with it. The actors spoke their awful lines, the choir sang their awful songs and the dancers cavorted. I avoided looking at Flora when it was time for the Leaf Dance. I just stared at the sky, shook my acorns and waved my branches about. So I don't know how she got on with her fluttering.

After the Leaf Dance, I trundled offstage. Marion and Robin were waiting to go on, together with the handmaidens and the Merry Men, but they had to wait for the leaves to get off.

'Honestly,' said Charlotte. 'What on earth does Flora Ferguson look like?'

'She said her mum made it,' said Wendy.

'Looks like it,' said Charlotte. 'It's gross.'

I looked across the stage at Flora, who was as red as a beetroot and sweating a lot, but clearly relieved the ordeal was over for now.

'Totally gross,' sneered Charlotte, again.

Suddenly, I was mad. Suddenly, I didn't care if her socks sparkled.

'Why don't you just shut up, Charlotte?' I said.

She looked amazed. I've never been rude to her before. Her eyes went all flinty. She said, curtly:

'Why don't *you* shut up, Tim? You're just a tree.'

She was right, of course. I was.

Chapter Six

It was the big night. Mum and Dad were coming, with Kenny. They knew I was only a tree, of course. I'd finally told them. They went on about how the size of the part didn't matter, and we went through the whole thing about giving other children a chance. But I know they felt a bit sorry for me. For themselves, too. For years, they've basked in my reflected glory. Years of people coming up and complimenting them on my triumphant performances and saying I should go to stage school. They love it – although not enough to cough up the money and send me to one.

The performance was at seven o'clock. All the performers had to be there at six. I called for Flora so we could go together.

I rang the bell and waited on the doorstep. I didn't feel like I usually do on the night of the school play. Last year, when I was God, I walked on air. Not in a supernatural way, I hasten to add. I mean I was all churned up, excited and busting to get on stage and start thundering. I was a tiny bit nervous, but not much. I had a great part and I knew I'd be good. (And I was.) But this year, I felt a bit flat. The play was boring and there was nothing I could do about it because I was a tree.

Flora answered the door. She was eating an apple.

'Ready?' I said.

'Yes,' she said, spitting a chunk on my jacket. 'Sorry.'

'It's OK. Where's your mum?'

'Upstairs getting ready. It takes her a while. Mum! I'm off!'

'All right, darling!' shouted Mrs Ferguson from on high. 'I'll be there early to get a good seat. Good luck! Good luck, Tim!'

'Thanks, Mrs Ferguson,' I called.

Off we went.

'Nervous?' I said.

'I've got bats in my stomach,' said Flora, miserably.

'I thought it was butterflies.'

'It was, but bats came and ate them. This apple

is the first thing I've eaten all day.'

'Ah, don't worry. Who's going to notice you? You're only a dancer.' That came out sounding wrong. Mean. Rude. Just plain wrong. 'Sorry,' I added.

'It's OK. I don't want to be noticed.'

'Your mum will notice you, anyway. Won't she?'

'Mmm.'

'Look, I'm sorry. Anyway, *I* can't talk. Nobody'll notice me either. I'm a *tree*, for crying out loud. A massive disappointment for my many fans, but there it is.'

'*I'll* notice you, dahling,' said Flora, putting on a posh, actressy, mock-admiring voice. 'All that super, fabulous swishing you do. And your lovely, *lovely* acorns.'

'And my couplets, dahling,' I agreed, in rich, actorly tones. 'Don't forget them.'

'How could I? High spot of the play. Today a tree, tomorrow Hamlet, eh what?'

We were doing our daft old routine. But our hearts weren't really in it.

'Hey, Flora. Did you know one in five people in the world are Chinese?' I asked.

'They are?'

'Yep. There are five in our family. That means one of us must be Chinese. There's Mum, Dad, me, Kenny and our new baby, Ho Ma Chin. *I* think it's Kenny.'

I'd been saving this one for an emergency. She giggled a bit.

When we got to school, the face paints were all set out and the lights up and working. The backstage helpers were setting out the benches for the choir, and the orchestra was unpacking their instruments (drum, violin, three recorders and cymbal, if you're interested. Oh, and somebody's grandad on flugal horn.) Miss Joy was sorting the music, Miss Steffani was giving the leaf dancers green eyelids and Mrs Axworthy was putting programmes on chairs. There was no sign of Mr Cunningham. I asked Mr Huff where he was. Mr Huff said he'd gone off to collect the Mayor.

Huh? The Mayor was coming? This was new.

'I hear the Mayor's coming,' I said to Mrs Axworthy, on my way to the boy's toilets where I would green up my face, pull on my cap of boughs, climb into my trunk, drape my material foliage and add my accessories of acorns, bird's nest and wood pigeons.

'Yes,' said Mrs Axworthy, with a funny little tight smile. 'Mr Cunningham has friends in high places, it seems. The photographer from the newspaper's coming, too.'

'Golly,' I said. 'It had better be good then.'

'Yes,' agreed Mrs Axworthy, with a sigh. 'Let us hope so.'

It wouldn't be. We both knew that.

I decided not to tell Flora about the Mayor or the photographer. She was looking sick enough already. We didn't get time to talk anyway. I had to tree up and she had to queue for green eyelids.

James Shawcross was in the boy's toilets. He already had his hat and shirt on and was hauling up his sister Shirley's tights. As I've already told you, they were too short and gave him trouble.

'Problems?' I said.

'It's the elastic in the waistband,' he said. He talks almost normally when he's not acting, which is weird. A bit reedy, that's all. 'It's gone all loose.'

'Tie a knot in it,' I advised.

'I'm not sure it's long enough.'

'Try breathing in.'

He tried breathing in. After a lot of fiddling,

he finally got enough surplus to tie a knot.

'How's that feel?' I asked, as I pinned on my acorns and adjusted my wood pigeons.

'Like I'm cut in two.'

'Show business, eh?' I said.

Then the Merry Men came barging in with their carriers, all loud and overexcited, and we mucked about a bit and one of the sinks overflowed and Rakesh's bow snapped in half and Mr Huff came in and told us off.

Then we had to go and wait with the rest of the cast in Blue Class, because the audience was beginning to arrive and we didn't want people to see us in our glorious costumes. It would spoil the surprise.

Old Mr Turnbull had the unenviable task of looking after us and making sure we didn't muck about. He tried to get us interested in a game of hangman, but nobody could concentrate. We could see the audience arriving through the glass bit of the door.

Flora's mum was one of the first. She wore a smart coat and lipstick. I watched her limp up to the front and station herself right in the middle of the front row. I turned around to Flora, who was sitting on a table in her leaf costume, looking white (apart from her green eyelids) and turning the pages of an old joke book she'd found on a shelf.

'Your mum's here,' I mouthed to her.

She nodded and went back to her book. I don't think it was a very good one. She certainly wasn't laughing, anyway. The rest of the girls were playing clapping games and practising their dance steps, but she wasn't joining in.

Nearly all the seats were taken when my family finally showed up. They had to sit at the very back, which was just as well. It meant they could leap out easily if Kenny played up, which he tends to do during school plays, violin recitals and weddings, particularly the quiet, emotional bits. I hoped they'd remembered to bring plenty of bananas, which we use to keep his mouth full.

Our school hall's got a reasonable stage, but there's no room behind and hardly any room at the sides. So all the dancers and people playing the smaller roles have to sit on the floor at the front. That included me, of course. If ever there was a small role, it was the tree.

Seven o'clock came. The hall was packed. Through the door, we could see all the mums and dads waving to each other and chatting and looking expectant. Mr Cunningham sat in the front row, next to Flora's mum. He had the Mayor with him, and a man with a camera, who I guess was from the paper. The Mayor had a huge, gold chain on. That was how I knew he was the Mayor. Either that, or a hip-hop artist.

The lights went down. As instructed, we all lined up at the door. The piano started to tinkle and the choir stood up. The curtains pulled back to reveal the painted backdrop of a woodland glade. Everyone went quiet apart from Kenny, who announced, very loudly into the silence:

'WANT 'NANA!'

I could hear mum shushing him and a rustling noise. Good. They had remembered to bring some.

The choir struck up with their first rilly-dilly greenwood-o type song. Mrs Axworthy appeared with her finger on her lips, and quietly and sensibly we filed through into the hall, where we took our allotted places. Most of us sat cross-legged on the floor below the stage. Well, I sat curl-legged because of my trunk. Robin and the Merry Men went and stood in the wings, ready for their entrance.

The first song was quite long, all about how merry everyone will beee when they drink a toast to Robin Hooood beneath the Greenwood Treeee. Except that the tree was nowhere to be seen because there wasn't enough room for me on stage in this scene, as Mrs Axworthy had predicted.

When it finally finished, James came on. Mrs Axworthy had tried to get him to bound, but James was a boy to whom bounding doesn't come naturally. He came in at a sort of shambling trot, accidentally dropped his bow, picked it up and launched into his opening bleat.

'*Well here I am Robin Hood hiding in the forest I wonder what I can eat tonight times are hard…*'

It was a long speech. Half-way through, a familiar voice from the back said, loudly: 'MORE 'NANA.'

And who could blame him?

Thankfully, Little John entered on page two, preventing Robin from delivering any more history. They did their fight and as always it looked like a nasty playground incident. Mr and Mrs Kite looked proud, though.

Time then for the entrance of the Merry Men. Each had to deliver a small, dull speech, introducing themselves. There were no jokes, and they hardly came across as people you'd like to be stuck in a lift with. The Mayor was looking at his watch.

Then there was a castle scene, with Prince John and the Sheriff of Nottingham discussing Robin Hood and how awful he was. Then Marion and her handmaidens joined them and there was more talk with extra squeals. Rachel's wimple caught on the scenery and came adrift, which caused a bit of mild interest. Then they all trooped off. The audience is supposed to clap at the end of every scene, but Prince John tripped over his curtain, so they laughed instead.

Then we were back in Sherwood again, with a load of oppressed peasants moaning about their lot. There came the sound of snoring from behind me. I glanced round. The Mayor was asleep. Next to him, Mr Cunningham was staring straight ahead with his arms folded. He looked a bit grim.

'WHAT'S 'AT BOY DOIN'?' demanded Kenny from the back.

I didn't know what he was on about. As far as I could see, nobody on stage was doing anything apart from standing around droning on about the right to gather kindling.

At this point, I tried to catch Flora's eye. She was sitting with the rest of the leaves in the row behind me, right at the far end, staring down at her big feet.

'NO!' Kenny advised us all as the peasants finally trailed off, to ill-deserved applause. 'NO! NO MORE 'NANA!'

Next came the bit where Robin Hood is in disguise and talks to the Sheriff of Nottingham. James's disguise consisted of leaving his hat off and putting a cloak on. Everyone but the Sheriff could clearly see it was Robin. His sheep voice alone gave him away. But at least Kenny had stopped heckling.

Probably dozed off, like the Mayor.

Chapter Seven

I was getting pins and needles by now, so I was very relieved when the next song began. It was a sad one about peasant poverty, and my cue to go on stage. At last! My acting debut. I heaved myself upright, shedding acorns. I adjusted my bird's nest, made sure my wood pigeons were properly attached and climbed up the steps to the stage, where I took up a commanding central position and raised my smoke-alarm hardened arms. The lights were shining directly in my eyes. I couldn't see Mum or Dad, but I heard Kenny all right. He wasn't asleep after all.

'TIM!' he roared, wild with excitement. 'TIM! TIM! TIM! TIM! TIM TWEEE!'

The audience laughed indulgently. Ever the professional, I ignored him and concentrated on the job in hand.

The peasants came back on and formed a tight circle around my trunk. It has to be tight because there are only four of them. The orchestra struck up with something skippy and the peasants linked hands and squeezed around me, while I swished. Jason trod on my foot, I lost a couple more acorns and my waving elbow caught Zoe in the eye, but we've done it worse. We got a polite clap, anyway, and loud, appreciative cries of 'TWEEE! TWEEE! TIM TWEEEEEE!' from Kenny.

The Mayor was still asleep.

After the dance, I remained on stage and continued to enrich the world with my tree presence while Robin and the boys came back on and gave the peasants some money, which they'd robbed from the rich. Then there was a sort of celebration in mime, where they all pretended to drink mead and tried to look like they were having a good time. That's when I said my first lot of rhyming couplets.

Right on cue, I swished my branches and declared, in a loud, clear, only *faintly* bored voice, with a hint of twig:

'*So Robin and his merry men*
As happy as can be
Now spend a night carousing
Beneath the greenwood tree.

'Ladies and gentlemen, there will now be a short interval. Drinks and raffle tickets are on sale in the foyer. All proceeds will go towards a new climbing dragon in the infant playground.'

Mrs Axworthy had told me to say that.

Everyone clapped, James dropped his bow again, the Mayor woke up, chairs were pushed back and the parents fled to the foyer for a strong drink. Wine is one pound a glass. Mum says it's like vinegar, although that never stops her drinking it, I notice.

Flora's mum was a bit slower than the rest. She gave me a thumbs-up sign as I came shuffling offstage and mouthed: 'Wonderful!'

She's really nice, actually, pretending to enjoy herself even though Flora hadn't done her dance yet. I looked around for Flora, but she wasn't there. Probably being sick in the girl's toilets, where I'm not allowed to go.

The cast isn't allowed in the foyer at the interval. Mrs Axworthy says it's unprofessional. So I went back to Blue Class with everyone else and mucked about.

Then it was time for Act Two.

There we all were, back from the interval, house lights off, orchestra and choir revving up for their next song, which is all about the Fayre and how everyone would be there and they wouldn't have a care and so on.

"NANA!' shouted Kenny when they finally sat down, and I couldn't agree more.

Next came the archery contest. After a lot of failed experimentation with elastic and consultation with the other teachers, Mrs Axworthy had decided to have the competing archers shoot offstage. Then Friar Tuck rushes in holding a dartboard with Robin's arrow miraculously sticking out from the bull's-eye. I told her that in a modern age of dazzling special effects it might seem a bit feeble, but she just looked tired and said it would have to do.

In every version of *Robin Hood* I've ever seen, the archery contest is the best bit. Not in ours, though. There were so many people on stage you couldn't really see what was going on. The entire cast were up there, milling about. Everyone except the leaf dancers and the tree and King Richard the Lionheart, who doesn't show up until the very end, when he says all of three lines. (Tariq was King Richard. Like me, he had drawn the short straw. Though he claimed he didn't care.)

James and the Merry Men had been practising shooting arrows ever since they got their bows, but they still weren't any good. The trouble was, the bows were too flimsy and the arrows hardly ever made it offstage. Dillon managed it once, in rehearsal, but it was a fluke. Miss Steffani was in despair.

Tonight was no better than usual. Little John's arrow went sideways into the orchestra and Will Scarlet's broke in half before he even fired it. Dillon's stuck in the stage curtains. It didn't matter so much for them, of course, but Robin is a different matter. He's supposed to be a great marksman. His arrow is supposed to fly straight and true. In James's hands, it rarely left the bow.

Everyone crossed fingers and hoped for the best as James raised his bow and Billy Tarbuck from Year Three played a dramatic roll on the drum. *Yeah*! We thought. *Come on, James. Concentrate. Let that arrow fly*!

He pulled back the string. The drum roll stopped. A tense silence fell.

'WHAT'S 'AT FUNNY BOY DOIN'?' demanded Kenny, into the silence.

James let go and the arrow flopped on the stage in front of him, same as usual. The audience pretended not to notice and acted duly amazed when it turned up in the bull's-eye brought on by Friar Tuck. A couple of the dads even cheered. Well, you had to laugh. Mr Cunningham didn't, though.

I looked over at Flora, to see what she thought. She didn't look up. She was still staring down at her feet.

Did I mention the Mayor was asleep again?

After the contest comes the scene where Robin declares his love for Marion. James tends to speed up during this, like a sheep in a hurry, anxious to be over the hills and away to pastures new. Charlotte does a lot of hair tossing. Why had I never noticed her simpering before? I can't believe I used to like her. I must have been dazzled by her socks. Stars in my eyes, I suppose.

After the love scene, in which James managed to drop his bow yet again, there was another tedious bit with Prince John and the Sheriff of Nottingham. And then –

Me again. Up I got and shuffled up the steps to my familiar position stage centre as the orchestra struck up for the next dance.

'TIM!' howled Kenny, completely out of order now. 'TIM! TIM! TIM! TIM! TIM! TIM!

TIM *TWEEEEE!*'

Any minute now, he would have to be forcibly removed, I could tell.

Charlotte, Wendy, Shanti and Fatima came skipping on and began circling me with linked hands. I began madly waving my foliage.

The dance didn't go too badly, although one of my wood pigeons slipped and my shoulder nest was beginning to give me a rash on the chin. Fatima's shoe came flying off during the second circuit and she had to carry on with one bare foot. I saw Charlotte glaring daggers at the poor girl.

After the dance, they did a bit of talking and squealing about Robin, then ran off. And now it was time for the Leaf Dance.

The leaves all clambered to their feet and filed on stage. I looked down at the front row. Mrs Ferguson was sitting up eagerly, eyes glued to her big, green daughter. I noticed that her fingers were crossed.

Flora was last on. She tripped a bit, on the top step. Head bowed, hair out, she plodded to her place on stage like she was approaching the gallows. Poor Flora. She knelt down at the back, like she was supposed to do, along with the rest of the leaves.

The leaf music is recorded. Miss Steffani couldn't get the tape recorder to work, so the leaves had to keep on kneeling while Miss Joy came and helped her. I did a bit of extra swishing to fill in. I could see the leaves getting uncomfortable. The audience was very patient. I could hear Kenny's echoing voice out in the foyer, still screaming, 'TIM!' Dad had taken him out, then.

Finally, they got the tape recorder working. Clearly relieved, the girls rose to their feet and began fluttering. Out of the corner of my eye,

I saw Flora dutifully leaping about with the rest of them.

I caught a glimpse of her mum in the front row. She was on the edge of her seat, craning to see. She had a job, because Flora was doing most of her fluttering behind me, and my foliage tended to block her out.

Finally, it was over. The music stopped and the leaves fell to the ground, where they would presumably become mulch. The audience applauded. I bowed in a majestic, tree-like way and allowed my branches to droop. That was a relief. High-level swishing hurts after a while, despite my smoke-alarm arms.

Now, this is where it all went seriously pear shaped.

There had already been a few instances in the play where things had gone a bit wrong – Fatima's shoe and Josh's trip up and James continually dropping his bow and the archery contest debacle – but none of them were serious.

This was. I'll tell you what happened.

The leaves were attempting to get offstage. There was a bit of a bottleneck at the steps, as always. At this point, I'm supposed to shuffle off and wait in the wings to make space for the next bit. Robin and the Merry Men and Marion and her lot are meant to come on and talk about the future of Merrie Englande.

I looked over into the wings to make sure Charlotte and James were ready to make their entrance. But there seemed to be a bit of a problem. There was a lot of milling around and anxious whispering. Everyone had their back to the stage. Whatever was going on?

Mrs Axworthy's face turned to me. She was frantically mouthing something, but I couldn't make it out. Shanti moved to one side, and I suddenly saw what had happened. James was standing there, eyes wide with anxiety, clutching desperately at his middle.

Ahhhh! Disaster! His tights had given way! The boy had dropped his bow once too often. The elastic had finally snapped under the strain!

The leaves were nearly all offstage now, leaving me alone in the spotlight. Except that Flora hadn't quite managed to get down the steps. She desperately wanted to, but there was still a bit of a blockage.

The audience was getting restless. Nothing was happening. In the wings, Mrs Axworthy was making desperate, circular motions with her hand. I know what this means. It means do something, for crying out loud. Improvise. Do something, say something, *anything*! Whatever happens, keep going, for the show must go on. So I did.

'Hey, Leaf!' I said. I pointed a branch at Flora.

She was just about to step down off the stage. She hesitated and turned her red, agonised face to me.

I felt for her, but I ploughed on. 'Yes, you!' I said, in my twiggy voice. 'I want to talk to you.'

For a moment, I thought she would ignore me and just scuttle down the steps, leaving me high and dry. But she didn't. She said, rather croakily:

'Who, me?'

'See any other leaves around here? What are you, the last leaf of autumn?'

'Yes,' croaked Flora. She cleared her throat, and then said it again, more clearly. 'Ahem. Yes. That'd be me.'

'What are you doing after the show, Leaf?' I asked.

'I'm not sure yet,' said Flora, adding, after a moment, 'But I can't be-leaf it's not flutter.'

A play on the name of a well-known margarine product. Not bad, on the spur of the moment. It brought an appreciative rumble of laughter from the audience, who were starved of humour.

'Me, I'm off to find my roots,' I said. That got a laugh, too. Encouraged, I went on.

'I auditioned for Robin, you know,' I said. 'I was tree-mendously disappointed when I heard I was a tree. Although I have to say this costume's better than the one they made me wear in the last play.'

'Which was?'

'They made me dress up as a hunk of bread filled with cheese and pickle and tomato and lettuce and cucumber and mayonnaise. I did it because it sounded like a *big roll*.'

That went down well.

'You should audition for *Star Trek*,' said Flora, when the laughter subsided. 'You could go as the captain's log.'

So did that.

Flora moved away from the steps and came to stand nearer, so we didn't have to shout.

'How about you?' I asked. 'Did you try for Marion?'

'Oh no. I wanted to be a leaf. I love being a leaf, me. I'm a leaf in all the plays. When I heard I was a leaf again, I could hardly be-leaf my ears.'

Over in the wings I could see Mrs Axworthy frantically beckoning to Mr Huff, who was at the front of the hall lounging against the wall, watching us and grinning a bit. He saw her tragic face and went to the side of the stage to have a whispered consultation. Then he went hurrying off somewhere. James was still grimly hanging on to his modesty. The handmaidens were looking anxious, hopping about impatiently and wringing their hands. Charlotte, I noticed, was looking furious. The crisis was far from over.

'Know any more tree jokes, Leaf?' I asked.

'A couple,' said Flora. She was gaining in confidence now and opening her mouth more. Her braces flashed in the spotlight. 'What d'you call a tree who listens to other trees' conversation?'

'I don't know. What *do* you call a tree who listens to other trees' conversation?'

'A leaves-dropper.'

'Boom-boom!' we both went, throwing out our arms in time-honoured comic fashion.

The audience groaned, but in a good way. Even the Mayor joined in. He was awake, for once.

'And then, of course,' continued Flora, on a roll now, 'there's the one about the couple of blokes who see a sign saying: Tree Fellers Wanted. They didn't get the job because there was only two of them.'

This went down well, too.

'Have you heard the story about the three eggs I've got in my bird's nest?' I asked.

We had to keep the pace up. Out of the corner of my eye, I saw Mr Huff returning from his mission. In his hand was a large safety pin.

'No,' said Flora. 'I haven't heard the story about the three eggs.'

'Two bad,' I said. We looked at each other, spread our arms and said, 'Boom-boom!' again.

There was more laughter and spontaneous clapping. From the back of the hall I heard the triumphant howl of 'TWEE! TIM! TWEE!' Kenny was back, then.

'I think I'll take a bough,' said Flora, plucking one of the branches from my swimming cap and waving it round before bowing deeply, making sure people got it.

'Hey!' I said, pretending to be cross. 'Fingers off the foliage! I have enough trouble with these wood pigeons. Have you met my pigeons?'

'No, but I'd so love to be introduced.'

'This one's called Cheep, because he was going cheap.' Groans and chuckles from the audience. 'And,' I went on, 'this one's called Free.'

'Because you got him free?'

'No, because his brothers, One and Two, had already been sold. Talking about brothers, did you know that one in five people are Chinese? Robin Hood was telling me there are five people in his family, so one of them must be Chinese. There's Mrs Hood, Mr Hood, his big brother Colin Hood and his little brother Ho Ma Chin. Robin thinks it's Colin.'

It's my favourite joke of the moment, and I'd got it in. Hooray! The audience loved it, as they rightly should.

'Talking of Robin Hood,' said Flora, when things calmed down a bit, 'Did you hear about his pet bulldog, Gnasher? He's got crossed eyes, so Robin took him to the vet and...'

While she told the one about the heavy dog who has to be put down, I took another glance into the wings. Mrs Axworthy was bending over James's treacherous tights and doing something with the safety pin.

'"Whaaat?" said Robin. "Just because he's got crossed eyes?" "No, because he's really heavy",' ended Flora, and the audience erupted. People were cheering and clapping. It was the way she told it. It brought the roof down. The Mayor was shouting: 'Well done! Aye, that was a good one.'

I caught sight of Mrs Ferguson. She was just sitting with her mouth open. I think she was too shocked to clap, but I could tell how much she was enjoying Flora's performance because her eyes were all shiny. I think she was crying a bit. My mum does that too sometimes, especially when I'm something good, like God. I could hear Kenny informing everyone I was a twee, in case they weren't sure, but it didn't matter because it blended into the general sense of happy wellbeing.

In the wings, Mrs Axworthy was standing back from James, who was patting his waistline and nodding. Emergency over. It seemed that his tights were finally secured. Mrs Axworthy looked over at me and Flora, gave a huge, encouraging smile and did the thumbs-up sign.

It was over. We had done it. The play could go on.

'Well,' I said. 'I think they've had enough of us, Leaf. Time to get on with the play. It was nice knowing you.'

'Same here, Tree,' said Flora. 'Let's take another bough.'

She removed another one from my head, and we both bowed low. Then she hurried off down the steps and went to join the others.

Chapter Eight

Everything got back on track after that. Marion and Robin came back onstage, together with the handmaidens and delivered the final history lecture. Then they all went off to get smartened up for the wedding. King Richard then arrived and delivered his thankless lines. I could tell he had cramp from sitting cross-legged so long. He could hardly stand upright, poor kid, and kept bending down to massage his shins. What was really sad, about a hundred members of his family had showed up to watch him.

Then I shuffled back on and delivered my final rhyming couplets. I didn't joke them up or anything, although I think people were expecting me to. But you don't mess with Mr Cunningham's lines. I said them as written.

Then it was the ding-dong wedding song, during which everyone proceeds onto the stage to take their bow. I was there already, of course, but I had to shuffle to the side to make way for the important characters, like Marion and Robin in their wedding gear (same clothes plus fake flowers).

I took my bow right at the end, after King Richard. Without wishing to sound immodest, I think I got a pretty good reception.

There wasn't room for the leaf dancers on stage, so they just stood up and took a bow from the floor. They got a huge clap. I think – no, I *know* – it was because of Flora. She looked a bit sheepish, but she was smiling, despite her braces.

Mr Cunningham stood up and made a brief speech, thanking the teachers for their hard work. They all got flowers except for Mr Huff, who got chocolates. I think he should have got one of those hats with corks on, like Australians wear. Although he's probably got one already.

Mr Cunningham didn't mention that he'd written the play. Not at that point, anyway.

Then it was the raffle. Ben's dad got a bottle of sherry, Zoe's grandma got a Gangsta Rap CD, Tariq's uncle got a set of useful cooking oils and, believe it or not, my very own mother got a box of Quality Street! Result!

The photographer from the paper took some

pictures, then rushed off home. And that was it. It was all over.

We went tearing back into Blue Class, where we screamed mindlessly and ran around for two minutes. The girls hugged each other and the boys clapped each other on the back. It was such a relief to get it over. Then we all took off for the toilets, where we removed our costumes and put our normal clothes back on. Some people carefully folded their stuff and put it into carrier bags to take home, but I didn't. I dumped my tree bits into the bin. I didn't think I'd be needing them again. Although I kept a wood pigeon as a souvenir.

James was in the toilets, wincing as he removed his rogue tights. The safety pin was sticking in, he said.

'Bad luck the elastic went like that,' I said, sympathetically.

'Yes,' said James. 'Good thing it happened offstage, though.'

'I bet you're glad you're not a girl,' I said. 'They must get troubles like that all the time.' Well, they would if they were three-miles tall.

'Too right,' said James, pulling on his jeans and hurling the tights in a corner.

'Well done, anyway,' I said. 'You were good.'

'Thanks,' said James. 'So were you, Tim. Amazing, actually, what you did.'

'Naah,' I said, with a modest shrug. 'Naah. I was just a tree.'

I went to find my parents. The entrance hall was full of people talking. I saw Flora's mum standing in a corner, being congratulated by Mr and Mrs Shawcross and the Kites. There was no sign of Flora, who must still be in the girl's toilets removing her complicated costume.

'Quite the little comedienne, your Flora,' Mr Shawcross was saying. 'Had me in fits. She's a natural. Great comic timing.'

'And what a lovely costume,' added Mrs Kite. 'Did you make it yourself?'

Mr Cunningham was standing with the Mayor. I heard them talking as I squeezed by.

'So you wrote it yourself, you say?' the Mayor was saying.

'Yes,' admitted Mr Cunningham. 'I thought I'd have a crack this year.'

'Very good, very good. Plenty of hard facts in there, eh? I tell you the bit that really took off, though. The bit with the tree and the girl playing the leaf. Got a career in stand-up, those two. Hey, there's the tree now. The man himself. Well done, lad. You had me chuckling I must say.'

'Thank you very much,' I said, politely.

'I was just telling your head teacher here that your scene was the one that stood out. Should have been more bits like that.'

I flicked a glance at Mr Cunningham's face, said thanks again, then moved hastily on to join my family. Kenny was slumped on Dad's shoulder, all banana'd out. Mum was talking to Mrs Axworthy. They were both drinking wine. They looked up as I pushed my way towards them, graciously accepting people's congratulations on the way.

'Here he comes,' said Mrs Axworthy, fondly, ruffling my hair. 'What a hero. Can turn his hand to any part, Tim. What will I do without him when he leaves?'

'Don't talk about leaves,' I said, modestly but quite wittily, I thought. 'I've had enough of leaves for one evening.'

They both laughed. Mrs Axworthy gave me a wink and said, wryly, 'You and me both, kid.'

'Well done, son,' chipped in Dad. 'You made a grown man cry.'

Honestly. Can't he ever think of anything else to say?

'So, where's Flora?' said Mum. 'I want to congratulate her.'

'Still changing, I think.'

'Well, have you seen Mrs Ferguson? We're giving her a lift home, if you don't mind walking.'

'Fine,' I said. 'You go ahead. I'll wait for Flora.'

'Dad'll give you some money for chips. Ray, give him some money.'

'Thanks,' I said. 'OK, see you later.' I fancied a walk anyway. It had been hot in the tree costume. I needed to cool down.

The crowds were beginning to thin out now. James left with his parents, waving me a cheery goodbye. I really must stop calling him a sheep. The Merry Men and the handmaidens and the peasants and the choir members were leaving too, with their respective families. Tariq left, with his enormous tribe of doting relations. Charlotte went stalking past and didn't even look at me. I didn't expect congratulations for saving the day, but a goodbye would have been nice.

I still don't understand why I ever liked her.

Soon, there were only a few diehards left. The Kites came over to congratulate me on my performance, and so did Dillon's grandad, who has dreadlocks. He told me he wanted to hire me and Flora for the comedy act on his sixtieth. I think he was joking, but still. Then they went, along with the last couple of leaf dancers. Now there were only the teachers and me and the caretaker. Mr Cunningham had left to take the Mayor home. The teachers kept chatting to me and being nice, even Mr Huff, but I could tell they just wanted to go and flop in the staff room for ten minutes. I said I didn't mind if they had important marking to do, so they went, taking the last bottle of wine with them.

I waited alone in the foyer. Actually, the silence was quite nice.

Finally, Flora showed up. She had removed her green eyelids and pulled back her hair with the usual elastic band. Her costume was in her carrier bag, and she was back in her brown skirt and cardigan.

'Where were you?' I asked. 'You've missed all the fuss. Everyone wanted to congratulate you, but there was no sign.'

'I was throwing up in the toilets, if you must know,' said Flora.

'Really?' I was amazed. 'But why?'

'Fame takes it's toll, dahling,' she said, in actressy tones. Then added, in a normal voice, 'I get nervous, that's all. Do you think people noticed my braces much?'

'Nah,' I said. 'Anyway who cares? You were great.'

'*We* were great, you mean,' she said. 'I couldn't have done it on my own. Where's Mum?'

'Gone home in the car with my mum and dad. She said she'd see you later and to tell you that she's really proud.'

'She did? That's all right then.' She put on an American accent. 'Shall we hit the trail, pardner?'

'Yee-hah!' I agreed. 'Let's get them dogies rollin'!'

So we went. We walked out into the cool night. We went the long way, so we could call in at the chip shop.

'That's it, then,' I said, as we strolled along eating them. 'Our last play at Eddington Primary School. And I was a tree.'

'And I was a leaf,' said Flora.

We looked at each other, then we cracked up. We laughed so hard, we nearly cried. Then we helped ourselves to more chips.

'A tree,' I said, and exploded again.

'A leaf,' chortled Flora, through a mouthful of chips. Accidentally, she spat a bit of one on my sleeve. 'Sorry.'

'That's OK,' I said, wiping it off.

Then we linked arms and walked home.

A Word From the Author

I'll tell you why I wrote this story. At primary school, when I was six, we put on a production of *Hansel and Gretel*. I desperately wanted to play the witch but had to be a mouse. My only line was 'cheese'. Even my parents didn't seem impressed. I got over it and didn't think about it any more until I was all grown-up and went to see a production of one of my own plays brilliantly performed by a boys' prep school in Cambridge. They did a fantastic job in every way. But what I remember most is that they poked in an extra bit. It featured two trees, discussing being trees and basically bigging up their parts. As I had written it, the trees had eight rather uninspiring lines between them, written in rhyming couplets. They didn't even contain a joke, which was mean of me. However small the part is (mouse, tree, flower, footman, third stick from the left, whatever) it helps if there's just one good joke, so at least you get a laugh and a bit of recognition at the curtain call. So the trees beefed up their characters and added some jokes of their own. Or maybe the drama teacher wrote them? I don't know. All I know, is it was hilarious and I wish I'd thought of it.

It stayed in my mind. Being cast as a tree, although you know in your heart you are better than that. Bigging up your part. Hmmm. There was a story in that…